Marcius Denison Raymond

Sketch of Rev. Blackleach Burritt and related Stratford Families

Marcius Denison Raymond

Sketch of Rev. Blackleach Burritt and related Stratford Families

ISBN/EAN: 9783741124358

Manufactured in Europe, USA, Canada, Australia, Japa

Cover: Foto ©Andreas Hilbeck / pixelio.de

Manufactured and distributed by brebook publishing software
(www.brebook.com)

Marcius Denison Raymond

Sketch of Rev. Blackleach Burritt and related Stratford Families

OF

Tarrytown, N. Y.,

BEFORE THE

Fairfield County Historical Society,

At Bridgeport, Conn.,

Friday Evening, Feb. 19, 1892.

PUBLISHED BY

REV. BLACKLEACH BURRITT.

It may seem presumptuous for a resident of New York to appear before the Fairfield County Historical Society with a page of local history, and yet is it not fitting that Westchester Co., especially, should bring some offering as a tribute to the debt it owes, for ever since the days of Wouter Van Twiller, and William the Testy, and Antony Van Corlear, who essayed in vain with windy proclamations and his wonderful trumpet to stop the inroads of those terrible Yankees, the peaceful invasion has been going on, so that to erase the names of the sons of Fairfield from its annals, would make a blank on many of the most illustrious pages of its history. The son may well indeed turn back and crown his honored sire with laurels.

"There be of them that have left a name behind them, that their praises might be reported; and some there be which have left no memorial; who are perished, as though they had never been."

In a secluded spot on the eastern slope of the Green Mountains is the unmarked grave of a son of Stratford whose name well deserves to be illustrious in the annals of the County of Fairfield. A man of liberal culture, of more than ordinary gifts, a stalwart Patriot in the stormy days of the Revolution, a pioneer preacher of unusual power, of marked individuality and rugged character, of honorable ancestry, and with numerous and not less honorable posterity, such a man was Rev. Blackleach Burritt. The story of his life is not devoid of interest, and yet strange to relate, although here born, fitted for college, educated for the ministry, and within the borders of this county captured during the Revolution and taken to the notorious Sugar House Prison in New York, his name appears but once in your annals, in a brief note in the history of Stratford. But first of his ancestry:

THE BURRITTS

May not have had heraldic fame, but they were of the un-
crowned Kings of Welshland, whom even William the Conqueror did not find it easy to dethrone, and who when they
sailed away over the sea to the New World brought with them
not only their brave hearts and brawny arms, but their indom-
itable love of liberty as well.

Among those early of Stratford were William Burritt and
Elizabeth his wife. They are said to have been from Glamor-
ganshire, Wales, but the exact date of their arrival has not
been ascertained; quite possibly they had tarried for a time
somewhere else in New England before coming here. The only
place wherein William Burritt's name appears prior to the inventory of his estate, date of January 15, 1650-1, is in a mem-
orandum of the number of rods of fence the share of each
settler to build. The paper bears no date, but was of course
prior to his death. In the schedule of his estate he is spoken
of as "lately deceased." The amount of the inventory was
about £140. A very moderate heritage for the widow and her
children, of whom there were three, two sons and a daughter;
Stephen, John, and Mary, who is said to have married a Smith
at an early day and hence the numerous Smith family in
America.

The widow, Elizabeth Burritt, appears to have been a thrifty
and sagacious woman, controlling her own affairs and ordering
her household well. Though apparently not able to write her
own name, she made her mark all over the early town records
in more senses than one. She was buying more than selling
and evidently adding to her possessions. She apportioned
considerable real estate to her sons by conveyances dated
April 5, 1675, as follows: "To my loving and dutiful son,
John Burritt, of ye said place, an equal half of my whole
accommodations in Stratford aforesaid, being ye allotment and
interest of my deceased husband, Wm. Burritt, or by procure-
ment of myself and my children, excepting only ye home lot
and parcel of land at ye Fresh Pond, in ye old field, ye which
has already been contracted to Stephen Burritt," one of which
contractions being that "ye aforesid John Burritt should have

the parcel of land lying on "Quimby's Neck," &c. Stephen Burritt drew lot No. 40 in division of lands in 1671, and John Burritt No. 81.

Widow Burritt evidently made her home with her eldest son, Stephen. Her will is dated Sept. 2, 1681, and she probably died soon after.

Stephen Burritt, the eldest son, was in the list of Freemen at Stratford "8th month, 7th day 1669," a lot owner 1671, and confirmed by the General Court as Ensign of the Train Band at Stratford in 1672, appointed Lieutenant Jan. 17, 1675, and the Council at Hartford, date of Sept. 18, 1675, ordered that "The Dragoones from Fairfield County being come up, and Major Robert Treat sending to us to hasten them to their headquarters near Suckquackheeg, it has ordered that accordingly the Dragoones of Fairfield should forthwith march away up to Norwottag, and so to our army, under the conduct of Ensign Stephen Burritt, and join them in defence of the plantations up the river, and to kill and destroy all such Indian enemies as should assault them on the aforesaid plantations." Again, at a meeting of the Council of the Colony held Nov. 23, 1675, Stephen Burritt was appointed Commissary of the Army, so rapidly was he promoted. No wonder Hinman says, "he was a noted Indian fighter." Evidently a man of force, courage and resource, Ensign Stephen Burritt stands out a heroic figure on the pages of the history of Stratford. He was not only a brave soldier, but the old town records give evidence that he was a man of affairs. At the Town Meeting held Jan. 1, 1673, he was chosen Recorder, and his beautiful and character-like autograph which thereafter frequently appears on the Town Books, may well be the envy of any of his descendants. In 1689 he was appointed on a committee to assess damages for the changing of Black Creek into Mill River, by which one Robert Lane claimed to have been "damnified!" The same year he was chosen one of the Townsmen. In 1699 was an auditor of the accounts of the Town Treasurer, and also chairman of the committee on killing wolves. What a wolf killer that brave old Indian fighter must have been!

He held other offices of trust, and was in his day one of the very foremost citizens of Stratford. The inventory of his estate, dated March 4, 1697, shows a footing of £1,177 2s, which includes £3 6s, as the value of his "arms and ammunition." He had died January 24, 1697-8, according to the old tombstone, fortunately still preserved. It appears that this ancient memorial was recently discovered by Mr. Robert H. Russell in the footpath leading from his house to his garden. It was several inches under ground, and about 200 feet from the southeast corner of the old Congregational burying ground, where it was doubtless originally placed. It is believed that many years since it was taken from thence by some vandal hands, and used for a time as a step-stone. Mr. T. B. Fairchild, of Stratford, though not a descendant or of kindred, to his credit be it said, caused this memorial stone to be returned and reset.

He had married, Nov. 8, 1673, Sarah Nichols, the daughter of Isaac Nichols, a prominent Stratford family, one of her sisters having married Rev. Joseph Webb, and another Rev. Israel Chauncey, pastor of the Stratford church from 1665 to 1703, who was one of the founders of Yale College, and was chosen its first president, but declined the honor. By this marriage Stephen Burritt had seven children, as follows:

Elizabeth, born July 1, 1675; William, born March 29, 1677; (died young,) Peleg, (1st) born Oct. 5, 1679; Josiah, born 1681; Israel, born 1687; Charles, (1st) born 1690; Ephraim, (1st) born 1693.

Peleg Burritt (1st) married Sarah Benit, (sic) Dec. 5, 1705, and had issue: William, baptized Oct. 13, 1706; Daniel, (Bridgeport church records) 1708; Sarah, (Stratford town records) born July 20, 1712; Peleg, (Jr.,) born Jan. 8, 1720-1. Peleg Burritt, Sr., of Stratford, deeded lands to his son Peleg Jr., at Ripton Parish, including forty acres on Walnut Hill, "excepting only my own new dwelling house," date of April 25, 1746. He had sold land on Snake Brook, to Richard Nichols, April 27, 1713. Date of his death not ascertained. Sarah, wife of Peleg, united with the church at Stratfield in December, 1709.

Of the other sons of Ensign Stephen Burritt, Josiah was one of the proprietors of Newtown, 1710, and had numerous descendants there. He married Mary Peat, March 10, 1703, and had Elizabeth, baptized (Bridgeport church) July 23, 1704; Stephen, baptized (Bridgeport church) Feb. 10, 1706; Benjamin and Phoebe, (twins) born (Stratford town records), Jan. 29, 1708; William, born January, 1709, all of whom were of Newtown. Israel, 4th son of Ensign Stephen, married Sarah Coe, March 4, 1719, and is said to have settled in Durham. Charles, 5th son of Ensign Stephen, had Daniel, Israel, Charles and Elihu (1), who married and had among other children, Elihu (2), who had Elijah, Elizabeth, Emily, George and Elihu (3), distinguished as the "Learned Blacksmith," who was born at New Britain, Conn., Dec. 8, 1811, and whose fame is world wide. Charles Burritt took Freeman's oath at Stratford September, 1730. He and Mary his wife, were members of the Stratfield church, 1718. Daniel Burritt, son of Charles and Mary, his wife, died prior to his father, who by will dated Jan. 23, 1761, gave to the children of his son Daniel. The distribution of the estate of Daniel mentions the widow Comfort, daughters, Roxanna married Richard Hubbell 4th, Peninah, married Samuel Brinsmade, and Amelia, and sons Stephen, Rollins and Elijah Burritt. Elijah, though mentioned last, was probably the eldest, and probably not a son of the widow Comfort, but of a former wife, as there is good authority for saying—Stephen was his half brother. Elijah was born in 1743, it is the family tradition, on the site of his lifelong residence, which still stands, and appears good for another one hundred years. He was a man of fine form and presence, six feet in height, of uniformly good health, never sick until the last year of his life. He died Sep. 23, 1841, at the advanced age of ninety-eight years and six months. His life was one of great activity, his business embracing blacksmithing, buckskin leather dressing, and cooperage, as well as farming. He was overseer and agent for the Golden Hill Indians from A. D., 1812 to 1834, at a period when their numbers comprised quite a band. This rendered the distribution of the income of their small fund both delicate and difficult. By them he was looked up to as a father. He was a man of high character and intelligence, of the strictest integrity and religiously a strong Churchman. He retained his faculties unimpaired in a remarkable degree until the last, and from his intelligence and long life, he occupies in local history a peculiar position. In his younger years he was acquainted with the men and events of the earliest period. In his latest years, he reached down, and communicated his knowledge to men now living.

Isaac Sherman, Esq., says: "It was from him, (Mr. Burritt) that I derived much of the information I possess relative to the early settlers of Stratfield," (now Bridgeport), and which he has so well transmitted in his published recollections.

Elijah Burritt was thrice married. His first wife was Sarah Hall, daughter of John Hall, Stratfield, by whom he had one son and five daughters. viz;

1. Daniel, merchant. Bridgeport, known as Colonel Burritt, unmarried.

2. Comfort, died young.

3. Ann, married Ephraim Wheeler Sherman, and had issue, three sons and three daughters.

4. Hannah, married Silas Shelton, of Huntington, and had issue, two sons five daughters.*

5. Mercy, married Captain James Fayerweather, of Bridgeport.

6. Phoebe, married Captain Samuel Hawley, No. 2,335 in the Hawley family record.

---

*—Of these daughters, Elizabeth was a member of the family of her grandfather Burritt until her marriage to Captain George Latield. Their children are Harriet, married Dr. Joseph S. French, Charles Howard, married Susan Lobdell, Mary Burritt, married Edwin J. Nettleton. Another daughter Harriet, married Henry Bassett, and had one son, Frank H., who with his mother now own and occupy the old homestead of her Grandfather Burritt, Mrs. Lafield, aged seventy-eight years, and Mrs. Bassett, aged seventy-five years, were able to attend the meeting of the Historical Society, Feb. 19, 1892, and listened with much interest to the reading of this paper. The oldest daughter, Mary Shelton, who married Mr. F. Huge, was also represented by her daughter, Mary Burritt, who by contributions of her pen and pencil illustrates and perpetuates the history of the Ancestral Home which was erected in 1783, on the site occupied by Mr. Daniel Burritt, father of Elijah. A crayon picture of this house made by Mary Burritt Huge is hung upon the walls of the Historical Society, as a companion piece to the portrait of Mr. Burritt, painted by Edwin White, for Mr. and Mrs. B. T. Nichols. Mr. Nichols who was the survivor, at his death directed it given to the Historical Society.
                                                                        E. B. L., Feb. 1892.

Mr. Burritt married second, Sarah Fairchild, of Redding, Conn. Her only child was

7. Mary, married Barak T. Nichols.

His third marriage was to Sarah (Chappell) McLean. She had by her first marriage, Dr. John McLean, physician, Norwalk, Conn., and Sarah, who married George Wade, Bridgeport.

Stephen Burritt, son of Daniel, and half brother to Elijah Burritt, had his residence on Old Mill Green near the Mill Pond. He married Hannah Platt Avery, daughter of Rev. Elisha Avery, of Norwalk, Conn., and cousin of John S. Avery[*] and had Charlotte C., born 1797, died Aug. 8, 1837; Mary Ann, born 1799, died Dec. 21, 1820; and Stephen Elisha Avery, born Nov. 8, 1804, died April 1825. Stephen Burritt died 1815, aged sixty-two years; Hannah, his wife, died Oct. 25, 1843, aged eighty years. The children were all unmarried, and the grave marks of the entire family stand together in Pembroke cemetery.

Stephen Elisha Avery Burritt appears to have been a very bright and promising young man. He was graduated at Yale College in the class of 1824, when but nineteen years old. A class album of his, of remarkable interest, is in the possession of the Fairfield County Historical Society, donated by J. N. Ireland, Esq. The original contributions and selections show a high appreciation of young Burritt, and bear the signatures of such men as Judge Origen Storrs Seymour, Hon. Eliphalet T. Bulkeley, father of Governor Morgan G. Bulkeley, Linus Child, Ebenezer Jessup, Dr. Jeremiah T. Dennison, Benjamin D. Stillman, Esq., New York; Hamilton Murray, New York; Dr. Frederick J. Judson and Henry D. Sterling, (brother of Hon. D. H. Sterling,) of Bridgeport, and others of equal standing.

Ephraim's children were Eunice, Martha, Mary, Ephraim, Jr., Stephen, William, Abel and Lewis.

Daniel Burritt, son of Stephen, who was a son of Josiah, son of Ensign Stephen, probably married Sarah Collins, at New Milford, Feb. 8, 1756, and lived at Arlington, Vt., for

---

[*]Note.—John S. Avery occupied the Stephen Burritt place about 1840.

some years prior to the Revolution, when, being a Loyalist, he went to Canada and settled at Augusta, near Prescott, where he died aged ninety-three. Of his sons, Adoniram lived to be ninety-eight, Stephen, eighty-four, Daniel, Jr., eighty-seven, and Major upwards of ninety; a daughter, Lois lived to be ninety-three. Whether Toryism had anything to do with this extraordinary longevity is not recorded. Perhaps it was to give time for repentance. But there were many patriots among the Burritts, some of whom lived to be aged. Among those whose names appear on the list of Revolutionary soldiers in Connecticut are John, Philip, Abijah, Anthony, Charles, Elihu, Israel, Nathan, Abel, Eben, Stephen, William Burritt and others. Israel Burritt was from New Milford, and was commissioned as Lieutenant. Andrew Burritt, born 1741, who married Eunice Wells, Jan. 27, 1763, and was the great-grandfather of Oscar C. Burritt, of Hydeville, Vt., is also said to have been engaged in the Revolution. Some of the descendants of the daughters of the above Daniel Burritt, still reside at Arlington, Vt.

John Burritt, son of William and Elizabeth, and the younger brother of Ensign Stephen, as appears in the Stratford records was a lot owner as early as 1671. He married Deborah Barley, or Barlow, May 1, 1684, and had a son Joseph, born March 12, 1685, as the records show. Although Savage says in his Genealogical notes that John was unmarried, he appears to have been twice married, his second marriage having been with Hannah Fairchild, date of May 5, 1708. It is claimed that he had a son John, but that is doubtful, for Joseph is named as Administrator, and as sole heir of his father's estate, date of Oct. 3, 1727, the will having been filed Feb. 17, 1726-7. The inventory of the estate amounted to £1751.9s1d. Joseph Burritt made his will March 10, 1750: left widow Mary, sons William, John, Nathan, Samuel, daughters Deborah, wife of Jonas Thompson, Hannah, wife of Isaac Beach; also had Mary, born Sep. 22, 1721, and Ebenezer, born Dec. 18, 1728. This Joseph Burritt, son of John, was probably the ancestor of Joseph Burritt, born in Stratford in 1758, who married Sarah Ufford, and was the father of Joseph

Burritt, Jr., who died at Ithaca, N. Y., in 1858, aged ninety-four. He had married Asenath Curtiss, of Stratford, June 17, 1816, and left many descendants.

Peleg Burritt, Jr., born Jan. 7, 1719-20, married first (his second marriage is elsewhere noted) Elizabeth, daughter of Richard Blackleach, Jr., of Ripton Parish, date unknown, but evidently prior to Dec. 15, 1712, for on that date Richard Blackleach, Jr., conveyed land " to my son, Peleg Burritt, Jr., of said Stratford." He doubtless lived at Ripton Parish. There was a daughter born of this marriage named Mehitabel, after her grandmother, Mehitabel Laboree Burritt, and a son Blackleach Burritt, but the church records of Ripton Parish, prior to 1773, having been destroyed, and the family record of Peleg Burritt, Jr., having been lost at the time of the Wyoming Massacre, it has been found impossible to definitely ascertain the date of the marriage or the birth of either of these children. The birth of Blackleach Burritt has been placed by some as early as 1740, but as his father was then scarcely twenty years of age, it cannot be taken as even appropriately correct, especially in view of the fact that his sister's name precedes his in order of mention in the will of their grandfather Blackleach. Probably she was born about 1742, and he about 1744. As will be noticed he was cotemporary with the late Elijah Burritt, of Stratford, and not distantly related to him.

THE BLACKLEACH FAMILY.

The Blackleach family was early of Connecticut, John Blackleach, Jr., of Hartford, 1659, being perhaps the grandfather of Richard, Jr. Richard Sr , was of Stratford as soon as 1676 ; was a merchant, and is called Richard Blackleach, gentleman. In 1698, in the prosecution of his business, he was plaintiff in a suit against Mr. William Hoadley, merchant, of Branford, concerning some Negro Slaves delivered by him to the said Hoadley, to be paid for in corn, which was in the courts for several years, but in which he was finally successful. He was a high Churchman, but instead of carrying the Gospel to the Heathen on "Afric's golden sands," he evidently brought the Heathen to the Gospel! This experiment of his in the way of Evangelization, is in striking contrast with an earlier fact recorded of John Blackleach, (probably his father) who kept the ferry over the Housatonic river between Stratford and Milford, who in 1669, petitioned to be allowed to make known to the Indians, as he should have opportunity, "something of the knowledge of God." Richard Blackleach, Sr, died in 1731, aged seventy-six years.

Richard Blackleach, Jr., married Mehitabel Laboree, probably the widow of Dr. Laboree, Feb. 2, 1715-16, and had two children, Elizabeth, who married Peleg Burritt, Jr., and Sarah, who married Mr. Edward Jessup. Mehitabel Laboree Blackleach died Feb. 21, 1735. His will made Feb. 27, 1747, was recorded Oct. 2, 1750, and inventory filed April 28, 1751. The following is a transcript of the substance of it:

"I give unto Mehitabel Burritt, daughter of Peleg Burritt, Jr., of Stratford, one Silver Cup, two Silver Spoons, together with all my Movable Estate, provided she lives to ye age of eighteen years or marriage; but if she die before, I give said Movables unto Blackleach Burritt, ye son of Peleg Burritt, Jr." He also gave £5 to his daughter Sarah Jessup, wife of Edward Jessup of Fairfield, and £5 to each of her six children. He further gave "unto Blackleach Burritt, son of Peleg, Jr., and unto his heirs and assigns forever, all my land, meadow and buildings in said Stratford, being butted and bounded as appears of record." Ephraim Judson and Daniel Thompson were named as executors, and were given authority to sell land on Fawn Hill if necessary to pay the debts and bequests, and they did so sell lands to Peleg Burritt, Jr., date of March 5, 1753. The total inventory shows £1,051.3s7d, of which £850 was real estate. In the personal property was "one Silver Cup, holding near one pint, two Silver Spoons, and two dozen Silver Vest Buttons," valued altogether at £2.9s5d. And these were for Mehitabel, and something of personal property besides; quite a dower. Little is handed down in regard to this young lady, and it is not known whether or not she married. She is said to have been very handsome, and of a somewhat mercurial disposition.

The probate records of Fairfield show the final settlement

of the estate of Richard Blackleach to have taken place in
1758. The debits include a charge for going to Green's
Farms to pay the bequests to Mrs. Edward Jessup and her
children, and £16 paid out by the executors for the expenses
involved in a law suit, the records of which considerable research failed to disclose.

And so the lad Blackleach Burritt was made the heir to
quite an estate, the disposition of which, however, does not
fully appear. Nothing notable is known of his boyhood and
yorth except the stories of his acrobatic performances on the
roofs of buildings which he seemed to delight in, to the terror
of his step-mother, to whom he is said to have been much
attached. He does not appear to have been the traditional
goody, goody boy, who is expected to die young, but he had the
timber in him that men are made of. Aspiring after an education, he entered Yale College, where he graduated, as his
still well preserved diploma, an ancient parchment testifies,
in the class of 1765. An exciting incident of his college life
was the celebrated case of the poisoning of a large number
of the students. In answer to recent inquiry, Professor
Dexter, of Yale, gives the following version of the affair :

"The mysterious sickness at College occurred on April 14,
1764. A common rumor at the time, and later, imputed it to
poison administered by a French woman employed in the
College commons; but the more reasonable view held by
President Clapp was, that some students that were rebel-
lious against the food furnished in the commons, bribed the
French woman to put some strong physic into the food, in
the hope of breaking up the system."

In a sketch of Rev. Isaac Lewis, D. D., who was a native of
Stratford and a classmate of Blackleach Burritt, which appears in Sprague's Annals of the American Pulpit, the following account of that affair is given : "At that time the
whole College was poisoned through the villainy of certain
French neutrals. These fellows had taken mortal offense at
the conduct of a few wild students," and they meditated
"the most deadly revenge. To accomplish their purpose,
they contrived to visit the kitchen where the food of the stu-

dents was prepared and infused a large quantity of arsenic into one of the dishes that was to be placed before them. A deadly sickness came over all who partook of the food, and a few were so affected that they died shortly after."

Of Blackleach Burritt it is said that he was at that time engaged in nursing his sick chum, Samuel Mills. Another account says that he took a frugal meal of bread and milk on that occasion and so escaped being poisoned. Samuel Mills' father, Rev. Jedediah Mills, who was then and for many years the pastor of the church at Ripton Parish, in Stratford, was preaching in the pulpit when a messenger arrived from New Haven, and went first up into the pulpit, and then to Captain Burritt. Service was then dismissed, and both immediately went to New Haven. All of which is of interest as leading up to the fact that not long after this, Whitfield visited New Haven, and delivered a memorable discourse in the College chapel, that is said to have led to a great change in the current of Mr. Burritt's life, and which resulted in his uniting with the church in Yale College, date of Feb. 3, 1765, and led to the consecration of himself to the noble work of the Christian Ministry.

On graduating he pursued his theological studies with his venerable and able pastor, Rev. Jedediah Mills, of Ripton Parish, evidently in company with his classmates and companions of his boyhood, Samuel Mills and Isaac Lewis, for at a meeting of the Fairfield East Association, as appears in the old records now in the possession of Rev. Joel S. Ives, of Stratford, the Stated Clerk of that Association, held at Danbury on the last Tuesday of Feb'y, 1768, "Isaac Lewis, A. B., and Blackleach Burritt, A. B., presented themselves as Candidates for Examination to preach the Gospel. Their credentials being required, they offered the following, viz.: 'To the Revd. Asso'n convened at Danbury. Gent'm: Being detained by bodily Indisposition, I do hereby signify that Mr. Lewis and Mr. Burritt, the bearers, were sometime since recommended to us by Mr. Dagget, Pastor of a Church in New-Haven, and are in Good Standing with us in all things as becometh the Gospel. Mr. Jedediah Mills, Pas-

tor, Ripton, Feb'y 22, 1768.' Adjourned till to-morrow morning eleven o'clock. Met according to adjournment and proceeded to the examination of the Candidates as to their
Qualifications for the Work of the Ministry and then adjourned until to-morrow morning eight o'clock. Met Feb.
24, 1768, according to adjournment, and proceeded to com-
plete the examination of the aforementioned Candidates, as
to their Abilities natural & acquired, their Knowledge, Doctrinal and experimental, and finding them hopefully qualified
for the work of the ministry: do accordingly License them to
preach the Gospel, and recommend them to the Service of the
Churches wheresoever God in his providence shall call them."
Rev. Jedediah Mills, born 1697, was a son of Peter Mills, of
Windsor, Conn , born 1668 : he graduated at Yale, 1722, was
pastor of Ripton Parish from 1723-4'; a friend of Whitfield,
who commemorates him in his journal as "a dear man of God."
He died in 1776, greatly lamented, having retired from active
service three years previously. His son Samuel, who was a
classmate of Blackleach Burritt, was for some time pastor of
the Presbyterian Church in Bedford, Westchester County,
N. Y. Rev. Isaac Lewis, D. D., the other classmate referred
to, who was a native of Ripton Parish, Stratford, was located
many years at Wilton, was a Chaplain in the Continental
Army, 1776 ; and after the Revolution, was settled over the
Church at Old Greenwich, where Rev. Mr. Burritt, as will be
seen, was for a time located. He died Aug. 27, 1840, in his
ninety-fifth year.

And so Rev. Blackleach Burritt was regulary licensed to
preach. He had previously married Martha Wells, daughter
of Gideon and Eunice Wells, of Ripton Parish, at a date not
known, but probably soon after graduating from College, as
his second daughter was born Feb. 26, 1768. And as he
not only so married a descendant of the distinguished Colonial
Governor of Connecticut, Thomas Welles, but two of his
daughters were afterwards also united with kindred of that
name, it seems fitting to here give a brief lineage of that
noted family.

THE WELLES FAMILY

Is illustrious in the annals of this country, but as the head of one among the many different branches which here appeared at an early day, Thomas Welles, the distinguished Colonial Governor of Connecticut, stands out pre-eminent. It may be difficult to trace his direct connection with heraldic honors, or to those whose names were inscribed at Battle Abbey, by order of William the Conqueror, (the family tracings go back it is said to 794) but he was evidently of good family and so bore himself as to be well entitled to the kingly title of a man. Late investigations indicate that Thomas Welles was from Northamptonshire, where he was born in 1598. In the English Calendar of Colonial State Papers, is found, date of 1635, "Thomas Welles and Elizabeth l is wife Recusant, (i. e. Non-Conformists) in Rothwell, Northamptonshire." Articles of accusation were drawn up against him and he was warned to appear in the Court of Star Chamber to answer charges. He was admonished to answer " plene " under pain of being taken pro confesso. Was then warned to appear next court day to receive final judgment. Feb. 12, 1635, he had been ordered sentenced. As he then disappeared from Rothwell, having lost all of his property by confiscation, he doubtless at that time entered the service of his kinsman, Lord Saye and Sele, who protected all of the Puritans to the best of his ability.

"In the year 1635, John Winthrop arrived at Boston with a commission from Lord Saye & Sele, Lord Brooks and other noblemen interested in the Connecticut Patent, to erect a fort at the mouth of the Connecticut river. They sent men, ammunitions and two thousand pounds sterling, (Winthrop's Journal). Early in 1636, Lord Saye & Sele, with his Private Secretary Thomas Welles, came out to Saybrooke, but his Lordship discouraged by the gloomy aspect of everything about him, and not finding his golden dreams realized, returned to England, leaving his Secretary behind to encounter the dangers and difficulties of the then wilderness. Thomas Welles proceeded up the Connecticut river with his company as far as Wethersfield and Hartford.

Thomas Welles on his arrival in Connecticut, disclaimed "Arms," in compliance with the general custom, but that did not prevent his taking a prominent position at an early day in the affairs of the Colony, and from bravely counselling to take up arms against the warlike Pequots at that memorable Court of the Magistrates of whom he was one, held on the 7th day of May, 1637. He held the office of Magistrate for twenty-two years, and until his death. In 1639 was Treasurer of the Colony; in 1641. Secretary; in 1649, a Commissioner of the United Colonies; in 1654, Moderator of the General Court, and Deputy Governor; in 1655, Governor; in 1656-57, Deputy Governor; 1658, Governor, and in 1659 again Deputy Governor. Was considered one of the best writers in the Colony and most of the laws of that period were drafted by him. Was a man of affairs, and one of the largest taxpayers. He died at Wethersfield, Jan. 14, 1660, leaving a widow and seven children, four sons and three daughters, besides one son deceased.

John Welles, the eldest son of Governor Welles, born in Northamptonshire, 1621, came to this country with his father in 1636; was made a Freeman at Hartford, April 1, 1645; removed shortly after to Stratford in which he received his father's interest; was the Representative, 1656-7; Magistrate and Judge of Probate, in 1658. He died in 1659, aged thirty-eight years, leaving the following children: John, Thomas and Robert, (twins) Temperance, Samuel and Sarah. The widow, Elizabeth Welles, who was left by her husband's will "all that is due her in England and forty pounds to carry her there, if she chooses to go," married second, in 1663, John Willcockson, of Stratford.

John Welles, Jr., called Captain Welles in the Stratford records, was born at Stratford, in 1648, and was married to Mary Hollister, daughter of John Hollister, of Wethersfield, 1669. There were eight children, viz.: Mary, Thomas and Sarah, (twins) John, Comfort, Joseph, Elizabeth and Robert, all born in Stratford. John Welles, Jr., died Nov. 24, 1714.

Thomas Welles, eldest son of John Welles, Jr., born Jan. 2, 1674, was married about 1710, to Sarah, daughter of

Ephraim Stiles, of Stratford. There were nine children, as follows:

Bathsheba, born April 30, 1711; Ephraim, born Nov. 7, 1712; Comfort, born Sep. 15, 1714; Thomas, born Aug. 20, 1717; Gideon, born Nov. 12, 1719; Daniel, born May 19, 1722; Gurdon, born Feb. 3, 1724; Hezekiah, born July, 1732.

Thomas Welles was commonly known as Deacon Welles, being the first of that name to hold that office in the old Stratford church.

Gideon Welles, son of Deacon Thomas, married Eunice (----) and lived at Ripton Parish, in Stratford, where she died Jan. 8, 1805, aged eighty-five, and he died Oct. 19, 1805, aged eighty-six years. His will, probated Nov. 2, 1805, on file in the Bridgeport records, gives to his daughters Eunice Welles, who had married Simeon Hamilton, June 4, 1794;

Ruth Welles, who had married Timothy Hatch, Nov. 28, 1782;

Diantha Welles, who had married John Ayers, Dec 1, 1782;

Blackleach Burritt, Jr., son of my daughter (deceased,) Martha Burritt;

Each five pounds'; while the real estate was divided between his sons, Stiles, Gideon, Jr., and Robert Welles, all of Ripton Parish. Robert Welles married Anna Wheeler, Dec. 9, 1779. The marriages of the other sons do not appear.

Hezekiah Welles, the youngest son of Deacon Thomas, was married at Stratford, about 1753, to Phebe Latin, and had five sons: David, Josiah, born about 1756, Gurdon, Abijah and Abner. She died at Ripton Parish, Jan. 2, 1812, aged ninety years. Hezekiah was a Sergt. in Capt. Edward Barnard's company in the French war, 1759. He is believed to have removed to New Milford. His son, Josiah, married Prudence Leavenworth, at Ripton Parish, Jan. 13, 1776, and had a son, James, born 1780, who married at DeRuyter, Madison County, N. Y., Oct. 1802, Prudence, daughter of Rev. Blackleach Burritt.

Gurdon Welles, third son of Hezekiah, born Feb. 28, 1758, in Ripton Parish, was there married March 1, 1792, to Sarah, daughter of Rev. Blackleach Burritt.

The Fairfield East Association, which licensed Mr. Burritt, recommended him to the church at Ridgebury, as a worthy and proper person, and the records show him to have been there for a short period, from April 8, 1768, the predecessor of Rev. Samuel Camp, who was ordained there in 1769. From then until 1772, there is no record of him, but he is believed to have been at New Milford, Conn., where there were kindred of his wife's, and where there was a Separatist church, or at North Salem, Westchester, County, N. Y. As early as 1772, he appeared at Pound Ridge, in Westchester County, N. Y., and was the first recorded pastor of the Presbyterian church at that place. The records of the old Dutchess County Presbytery, of which he became a member, at a meeting held May 4, 1774, recommended the Congregation at Pound Ridge, to give a call to the Rev. Blackleach Burritt to settle among them in the work of the ministry. Whereupon a formal call was duly extended to him, and on June 15, 1774, an adjourned meeting of the Presbytery was held at that place for the purpose of his ordination. On the day following, after account of some preliminary business, and the formal ordaining of Rev. Mr. Burritt, the following record appears: "But inasmuch as there are certain difficulties subsisting in this Church and Congregation respecting Mr. Burritt's being settled over them, the Presbytery does not think proper to give Mr. Burritt the particular charge of this Congregation, as their stated Pastor, but do ordain him with reference to them, and appoint him to labor here in his Ministerial office for the space of one year." At the end of that year another remonstrance from aggrieved members of that congregation was presented to the Presbytery, but his friends were more powerful, and he was continued there for another year. A copy of the original protest is herewith presented, not only as a quaint and original document, but as giving occasion to show the trend of his religious thought.

To the Reverend Presbytery now Convened in Pound Ridge:

REV. SIRS: We the subscribers beg leave to show before you the Reasons why we are not willing the Rev. Mr. Burritt should not be introduct into the work of the Gospel Ministry in this place, which are as followeth, viz: The first & great reason is Because we in our opinions Look upon his principals in matters of a Religious Nature not to be Agreeable to the Directions, Rules & Precepts of the Gospel, & so consequently contrary to the Dictates of our Consciences, & also contrary to the Peace & good order of this place as to Ecclesiastical Enjoyments, & notwithstanding the Desirable qualities & Endowments which are Discoverable in the gentleman in other respects. As Sundry of us have signed for Mr. Burret's Salery, we stand ready to give the reasons severally when required. We desire to guard against a Party spirit. requesting the same of our fellow members of this community, humbly' imploring Divine assistance that we may all be brought to such conclution in unity as in this important afare shall be most conducive to God's glory & the public weal of this Ecclesiastical communite, is the earnest request of your most obedient and Humble Servts, the subscribers.

Pound Ridge, June 14. 1774.

Eb C. Brown.	Ebenezer Seymour,
David Fausher,	Nathaniel Fausher,
Amos Scofield,	Abraham Slason.
Enos Brown,	William Garnsey,
Joseph Scofield,	Timothy Bowton,
Ebenezer Bouton, Jr.,	Joseph Fanshaw,
David Dart,	
Joseph Seymour.	

To understand the causes of this protest it is only necessary to recall the fact that Mr. Burritt had imbided the spirit of Whitfield's preaching while in College, and that he had studied Theology under Rev. Jedediah Mills, who was a friend of Whitfield, and in favor of revivals, the new light movement. and less restrictions of Church and State, as it then existed in the Colony. That was evidently the reason of his early migration over the borders and into the larger ecclesiastical liberty which then obtained in the State of New York; but Pound Ridge being essentially a New England community, offered some resistance to his theological thesis. The opposition also embraced all there was of incipient toryism there, which his stalwart patriotism was sure to antagonize.

Mr. Burritt's official relations with the Church at Pound Ridge closed April 1, 1776, but his family appears to have remained a while longer. The well preserved tradition is, as stated by Rev. W. J. Cumming, in his History of the Westchester County Presbytery, that when Rev. Samuel Sackett, of Crompond, present Yorktown, N. Y., was so outspoken that he was obliged to seek safety in flight, Blackleach Burritt supplied his place. Miss Mary Lee, of a family long connected with the Church at Crompond, has the well remembered tradition, and says, "He was thought very much of as a Minister of the Gospel by the people of that place." He was doubtless there and in that vicinity for some two years after severing his relations with his previous charge.

MR. BURRITT'S CAPTURE.

As patriotism was a crowning glory to Rev. Mr. Burritt, so his capture was the dramatic event of his life. As already related, he bravely held the post of danger when others retired, but the Federal lines having been forced back so that it became desirable to use the Church and Parsonage at Crompond (present Yorktown) for military purposes, it became a necessity and duty to take his family to a place of greater safety. This probably occurred sometime in 1778. And then he and they seemed to disappear. His subsequent capture and incarceration in the old Sugar House Prison, was indeed a well authenticated tradition in every branch of his family, but where and when did the capture occur? As to the time, no date was mentioned, and as to the place, there was a wide divergence, some claiming that it was at White Plains, Westchester County, and others that it was on Long Island. Long continued research disproved both of these theories, but negations prove nothing. And *when* was the capture? Light unexpectedly flashed upon that query from a chance perusal of Washington Irving's biography, in which, in a quaint certificate to William Irving, testifying to his kindly interest in the welfare of patriot prisoners, and to which further reference will be made, he says that he was "prisoner in this city, (New York) as early in the war as June, 1779."

There was a clue and it was carefully followed up.

Where was he captured? That was the perplexing question. The search was continued as opportunity offered. The traditionary account seemed to place the scene near some navigable body of water.—the river or the sea. The Sound line in Westchester County was devastated and in the possession of the unrelenting loyalists—he certainly would not take his wife and children into the jaws of such a lion. Fairfield County only remained, but a careful scanning of its history gave no clue. Nothing in its recorded or unrecorded annals gave the first faint glimmer of light. But at last, patient waiting, patient looking, had its abundant reward, and the truth was made as clearly to appear as the sun in the heavens.

The following Tory account of Mr. Burritt's capture was found in Frank Moore's "Diary of the Revolution," credited to the New Hampshire Gazette of the issue of July 13, 1779, and it was the first discovery of the long looked for event. It led up to others that follow:

"June 19.—Yesterday morning about 4 o'clock 32 Refugees commanded by Capt. Bonnell and other officers landed at Greenwich, in Connecticut. A thick fog favored their entrance, and they marched through the town undiscovered; but the Rebel guard being at length alarmed, and imagining the Refugees to be more numerous than in fact they were, fled with precipitation before them, and so close was the pursuit that some were overtaken and secured. The inhabitants of the town refused to open their doors to the Refugees, and reduced them to the necessity of entering the windows; notwithstanding which they plundered the houses of nothing but arms and ammunition, their principal object being horned cattle, of which they brought off 38, also 4 horses and 10 or 12 prisoners. Among the latter is a most pestiferous Rebel Priest and preacher of sedition, who when taken swore that there was no firearms in his house, but upon his being cautioned against equivocation and threatened with the consequences which would result from persisting in it, his timid spouse produced his firelock and a cartouch box with eighteen rounds in it. The Refugees proceeded about six miles into the country collecting cattle, &c. On their return they were attacked by a body of Rebels, supposed to consist of about 150, with two field pieces, but they kept at such a distance that only one loyalist was wounded by their fire. Before the Refugees embarked they landed a field piece, which was of great service, and after engaging the Rebels two hours, during which time they expended all their ammunition, they got safe on board, and arrived at Oyster Bay about noon, with their cattle and prisoners. They were obliged to leave a number of the former on the Rebel shore for want of boats to bring them off."

No doubt this "pestiferous Priest" was Rev. Mr. Burritt, as the following account of the same affair taken from the files of Rivington's Royal Gazette, date of June 23, 1779, abundantly testifies:

"Some days ago a party of Rebels came over to Treadwell's farm, Long Island, conducted by Major Brush, and carried off Justice Hewlett and Capt. Young—since which the Refugees went over to Greenwich in Connecticut and returned with 13 prisoners, among whom is a *Presbyterian Parson* named Burritt, an egregious *Rebel* who has frequently taken arms, and is of great repute in the Colony ; 48 head of cattle, and 4 horses were brought in with the prisoners."

The following from the Connecticut Gazette of New London, issue of July 8, 1779, gives as will be seen, quite a different version of this Tory marauding expedition :

"New Haven, June 23.—Wednesday night last a party of the enemy from Long Island, landed at Green's Farms in Fairfield and plundered the house of Dr. Jessup of all they could carry off. The next night, (Thursday, June 17), a considerable party landed at Stamford, who before the inhabitants could collect in force, made prisoners of 8 or 10 persons, among whom was a Mr. Blackleach Burritt, an unordained preacher, and took off 30 or 40 head of cattle, which they got on board under cover of the fire of a privateer which landed close in under a point. *They likewise plundered all they could lay their hands on*, broke windows, &c., and committed many outrages."

It was easy to make the error of locating the raid at nearby Stamford : and as has already been noted, Mr. Burritt was a regulary ordained Minister of the Presbyterian Church.

Mr. Joel Hatch, Jr., nephew of Ruth Wells Hatch, sister of Mrs. Rev. Burritt, in his history of Sherburne, N. Y., says : " He was a zealous Whig during the Revolutionary War, often carrying his patriotism into his pulpit. A party of British soldiers, guided by Tories, surrounded his house in the night, took him prisoner, and hurried him into their boat, not allowing time to put on his clothes until they had him safe on board. They sailed immediately for New York, where he was confined most of the time in what was known as the Sugar House Prison."

The following dramatic account of the capture is by Mrs. D. E. Sackett, widow of the late Rev. H. A. Sackett, now of Cranford, N. J., an aged lady of rare gifts and culture, and a granddaughter of Mr. Burritt, as received from her mother, Diantha Burritt Gray, wife of John Gray, Jr., one of the original proprietors of Sherburne :

She says of Rev. Mr. Burritt that " He used often to take his musket into the pulpit for defence, and, if need be, for ready joining in offensive warfare." Again . "At the seizure, some privates burst into the room. Grandmother sprang between the raised bayonets and her husband, holding them at bay, (heroic daughter of the Revolution, Patriot mother, wife !) till an officer ordered 'them to desist. As they did not then allow him time enough, or had not enough of human kindness to let him dress, his poor wife followed, clothes in hand, begging a chance for him to put some on, which finally they granted with rough oaths. She then followed to the water pleading for her two cows. With 'Let the —— Rebel minister's wife have one of them!' she drove it back to her desolated home, grief for her lost husband and pity for her helpless children dividing her heart."

It is said that as Rev. Mr. Burritt, and the other prisoners were being hurried along toward the beach, the wives and children followed in the rear. When they had gone some dis-

tance an officer rode up to the little band, and urged them to
turn back, saying that they were being pursued by the Colon-
ists, and that if they failed to reach their boats before they
were overtaken by them, the women and children would be
between two fires: yet they followed on, and did not return,
but stood in silent protest against the robbery of their homes
though there were signs of battle near at hand. And so the
marauders sailed away with their prisoners and pillage, leaving devastation in their track. And this was the spot, this
the scene of the capture—Old Greenwich, modern Sea Beach.
There is still the old burying ground near which the Church
stood, and there in full view to the passing traveller, is the
old building, then the parsonage and the home of Mr. Burritt
and his family, from which he was so rudely taken. The records of the old church are missing for the Revolutionary
period, and the records of the Fairfield West Consociation do
not show Mr. Burritt's appointment there for the reason that
they were destroyed at the burning of Fairfield by the British
early in that year, but the town records of Greenwich bear
evidence to the fact that he was there, by his officiating at a
marriage there, date of February 10, 1779.

Soon after the capture, the disconsolate family removed to
Pound Ridge, Westchester County, N. Y., where they had
friends and were cared for during Mr. Burritt's imprisonment,
which was for a period of about fourteen months. The reference to Mr. Burritt in Irving's biography may pertinently be
here introduced. Mr. William Irving, the father of Washington Irving, had remained in trade in the city of New York
during the British occupation, and as the time for evacuation
drew near, evidently feeling that his situation was somewhat precarious, and fearing pro scription from the now
victorious Patriots, he obtained from Rev. Mr. Burritt the
following quaint certificate as a means of security :

" These may certify whom it may concern ; whether civil
or military officers, that Deacon William Irving, merchant in
this city, appeared to be friendly inclined to the liberties of
the United States & greatly lamented the egregious barbari-
ties practiced by her enemies on the unhappy sons of Liberty

that unhappily fell in their power—contributed largely to my
relief (who was a prisoner in this city as early in the war as
June, 1779), and was probably an instrument under God of
the preservation of my life, and by credible accounts I have
had from other prisoners, has been the means of the preservation of theirs also."

This document was signed "Blackleach Burritt, Minister
of the Gospel in the Presbyterian Church," and bears date
Nov. 15, 1783, just ten days before Washington and his army
entered the city in triumph.

The story of Mr. Burritt's relations with Mr. William Irving while in Prison are told by his granddaughter, Mrs. D.
E. Sackett, as follows :

"He discovered Mr. Burritt very low with prison fever, in
his miserable cell, and by personal influence had him given a
suitable place and medical care, and when he rallied Mr.
Irving looked after him each day in his convalescence. Mrs.
Irving also sent him a good bowl of coffee, in the bottom of
which was a cheering couplet painted ; and that grandfather
said did him about as much good as the comforting, strength-
ening beverage. And at last he rounded up his good deeds
by securing a release for him through an exchange of prisoners."

He used often to preach to his fellow prisoners, and was
known among the British officers and soldiers as the "Rebel
Priest." It is said that expecting to be released on a certain
Monday he prepared a specially spicy sermon for the Sunday
previous, which the officers in charge of the prison, knowing
his spirit and independence, were determined to prevent his
delivering, and accordingly released him on the Saturday
night before, ordering him to leave at once, which to his
regret, he was obliged to do."

The exact date of Mr. Burritt's release from prison is not
known, but the records of the Dutchess County Presbytery,
which at that time included a portion of Westchester County
as well, show that he was present at a meeting held Oct. 11,
1780, and officiated as clerk. The next mention made of him
is that at a meeting of the same body held Oct. 8, 1783,

" Presbytery was opened with a sermon by Mr. Burritt, from Psalm, 122:6. 'Pray for the peace of Jerusalem : they shall prosper that love thee.' " At this meeting the record says, " Mr. Burritt being reduced to low circumstances as to the comforts of this life and outward means of subsistence by reason of ye late war and otherwise, request ye advice of the Presbytery respecting ye means of relief, whereupon we agree to recommend him to the warmest charity of our Christian Brethren, and appoint ye clerk to draw up the commendation for the purpose." At the same meeting he and two others were appointed to spend one Sabbath each in missionary work in the lower parts of Westchester County.

Where Mr. Burritt was between 1780 and 1783, does not appear, but his family seems to have been a part of the time at least, at Ripton Parish, for he had a daughter born there in November, 1782. He is believed, however, to have been at Crompond a portion if not most of that period. The next reference to him is of the date of Dec. 1, 1783, when " the Presbytery met at Mr. Burritt's in the West Congregation in Fredricksburg," present town of Carmel, Putnam County, N. Y., having charge of the Mt. Gilead Church as well as the one at West Fredricksburg so called, and where he evidently resided. The site of the old log Church, (Mt. Gilead), where he preached, near Carmel, is still pointed out, and his memory is still cherished there.

On the death, June 5, 1784, of Rev. Samuel Sackett, for a long time except a brief period during the Revolution, pastor of the Church at Crompond, Rev. Mr. Burritt preached his funeral sermon. He was located at West Fredricksburg, or Red Mills—the present Mahopac Falls—for some three years, and it was there that a great affliction befel him in the death of his wife, in April, 1786. She was yet comparatively young, not more than 41 or 42,—the Church records of Stratford show her baptism Feb. 23, 1745—but the burdens of her life had not been light nor her tasks easy. She had come to be the mother of twelve children, and their care and the terrible strain of war times had been too great for her overtaxed powers. The youngest child and daughter was but an infant of a few weeks old when the mother gave it her last loving look, and fell asleep, another martyr to motherhood and duty, as was fitting a loyal daughter of her sire who bravely suffered confiscation and expatriation for conscience sake. The home was desolated by her death, and the children scattered, several of them going to live for a time with their kindred at Ripton Parish. On the 10th of May following, 1786, Mr. Burritt was present at a meeting of the Presbytery, but no further record is made of him until May 8, 1794, when his name was dropped from the rolls as being then of Vermont.

The following mention of him is copied from the Court Records of Fairfield County, book of Executions, date of Nov. 30, 1789:

To the Constables and Sheriff of the County of Fairfield:

"Whereas, Elisha Mills, of Huntington, recovered judgment against Blackleach Burritt, late of New Fairfield, in said County, and now an absent and absconding debtor and gone to parts unknown, before the County Court holden at Danbury within the County aforesaid on the 3d Tuesday of November, 1789, for the sum of £59.19s.6d. lawful money debt, and the sum of £2.10 costs, whereof execution remains to be done hereon, therefore by the authority of the State of Connecticut, you are commanded to levy on the goods, chattels and lands of the said Burritt as the law directs." &c., and if they were not sufficient to satisfy in full the debt and costs, then the said officers were "commanded to take the body of the said Burritt and him commit unto the keeper of the gaol in Fairfield County aforesaid," and there to keep him "until he pay unto the said Mills the full sum aforementioned," with fees, &c. And so this Veteran Patriot Pastor, who had suffered imprisonment for devotion to the cause of his country, was in danger of being thrust into a common jail as a debtor!

The records show that the officer reported on Dec. 1, that Burritt could not be found—he was probably elsewhere too actively engaged in his Master's service to pay any attention to these proceedings—"or money or other valuable consider-

ation," but that he had levied upon a tract of land in Huntington, Ripton Society, called the "Mohegan Rocks," (probably
the rocks are all there yet, though the last of the Mohegans
disappeared sometime since) containing nineteen and one-
half acres, which was appraised at £2 per acre, and that was
turned over to the said Mills towards the satisfaction of his
claim. It is interesting in this connection to state that the
town records of Stratford show that Blackleach Burritt pur-
chased that same piece of real estate, then called "the South
End of Mohegan Hills," of his father, Peleg Burritt, Jr., Jan.
5, 1765, paying therefor £112.10s. Evidently he had paid a
high price for it, or there had been great depreciation, or
Mills was a grasping monopolist. Perhaps something of each,
but Mr. Burritt evidently had considered the land as ample
security for the debt incurred.

An important fact disclosed by the foregoing, is that after
leaving West Fredricksburg, Mr. Burritt was for a time at
New Fairfield. Perhaps his second marriage, which was
with Deborah Wells, of the Long Island, Southold family, she
being a direct descendant of William Wells, one of the foremost men of that settlement, Recorder, Deputy to the General Court, and Sheriff of Suffolk County, N. Y., from 1665 to
1669—was while at New Fairfield, although she had kindred
at Wells, in Hamilton County, N. Y., not far from which, in
Greenfield, Saratoga County, he next appears, having been
the pioneer Pastor of a Church there as early as 1790, the
records showing that at a meeting held Sept. 12 of that year,
he was authorized to represent the Greenfield Church at a
convention "at Bennington, in the State of Vermont, the
present week." An old letter at hand also shows his residence
there during the early part of that year. The year following,
1791, Mr. Burritt is found at Duanesburgh, then of Albany
County, N. Y., where he is said to have formed a Church com-
posed mainly of Connecticut families, who tarried there for a
while, among whom were a brother, Stiles Welles, and a
sister, Mrs. Ruth Welles Hatch, of his first wife, and that was
probably what attracted him thither. In a letter dated at
Duanesburgh, Dec. 28, 1791, he writes: "Stiles Welles has

lately returned from Huntington." During the same period he was also ministering to a Church in the adjoining town of Florida, Montgomery County, N. Y. But this pioneer preacher could not long remain in any one place. The true spirit of the Pilgrims was in him, and impelled him on. The old records of the Church at Winhall, Bennington County, Vt, state that on Friday, Jan. 6, 1792, only about a week later than the date of the above quoted letter, he was there present and officiating. Again on the 11th of March following, the records show him to have been there, and so on from time to time during that year. The records then show that an Ecclesiastical Council was "convened at Winhall, on the 1st day of January, A. D., 1793, for the purpose of the Instalment of the Rev'd Blackleach Burritt to the Pastoral care of the Church and Congregation there," Rev. Robert Campbell, formerly of New Milford, Conn., officiating as moderator. It cannot be said to have been an inviting field for a preacher of his ability, but in passing that way he had been strongly urged to come; the offer of a farm to be given him affording a home for his large family doubtless may have influenced his decision, but he is quoted as saying with his characteristic self forgetfulness, "That if he did not go there perhaps nobody else would!" And so a log house was built for him and a log Church, and he became the first pastor of the Church in Winhall. The records show considerable additions to that Church under his ministrations, but it was a brief pastorate, and death soon came in between him and his family, and his people, and they were sorely bereft. The last mention of him in the records is of the date of "Lord's Day, January ye 5, 1794," when he officiated at a baptism. His health had evidently been broken, for in the letter referred to he says, "I have for a length of time been more feebled and disordered than usual." The privations and sufferings to which he was subjected as a prisoner and otherwise, during the Revolution, and subsequently as a pioneer preacher, had been a severe strain upon even his strong constitution, and he was stricken down by a prevailing malady which devastated New England during the summer and autumn of 1794. There was no cessation in those early days of struggle : no vacation for tired and overworked pastors : no palace cars to carry them away to famous watering places ; no beds of inglorious ease : but like good soldiers these Watchmen of Zion must die at their posts ; and so

> " Tranquil amidst alarms,"
> The summons found him " in the field.
> " A Veteran slumbering on his arms,
> Beneath his red cross shield."

The broken family was again scattered, never to be re-united. Some had already married, and others were elsewhere, yet of the fourteen children, twelve by the first marriage and two by the second,—a most interesting group--all survived. and all but two lived to have families. As evidencing their wide divergence, only two, those by the second marriage, died in the same place, although six of them and the widow, came soon afterwards to reside for a time in one place—Sherburne, Chenango County, N. Y., where Rev. Mr. Burritt had preached the first sermon to the Pioneers in 1792 ; and hence the interest of the writer in this story of his life.

In the absence of the family record, irrecoverably lost during some of the many removals, it has been a difficult task to gather up the somewhat imperfect data of his descendants here presented.

THE CHILDREN.

Eunice, named for her mother, appears to have been the eldest child, born at Ripton Parish, in 1766 She married a Mr. Hopkins, had children, and lived for a time prior to 1820, near Batavia, N. Y.

Melissa, the second child, was born Feb. 26, 1768, probably at Huntington, just two days after Mr. Burritt was licensed to preach. She married at Johnstown, N. Y., Oct. 9, 1791, James Raymond, a native of Kent, Conn., a descendant of Captain Richard Raymond from Essex, England, Freeman at Beverly, Mass., 1634, and afterwards of Norwalk and Saybrook, Conn. James Raymond was one of the original proprietors of Sherburne, N. Y., where he settled in 1792-3, his wife, Melissa Burritt Raymond, being one of the members of the first Congregational Church organized in that place July 6, 1794. She was a strong, independent character, and her son, Philander Raymond, was distinguished as one of the founders of the city of Toledo, Ohio, was the promoter, builder and superintendent of the celebrated Brady's Bend Iron Works, on the Alleghany river, Pennsylvania, and interested in other large enterprises. Melissa Burritt Raymond died at Brady's Bend, Pa., July 3, 1849, in her eighty-second year. Mrs. Rev. J. R. Preston, of Creighton, Nebraska, and E. F. Ensign, Esq., of Madison, O., are her grand-children.

Martha, (called Patsy) Burritt, was born Oct. 1770, and married about 1790. Elisha Gray, then of Florida, Montgomery County, N. Y. She removed with her husband, to Sherburne, N. Y., in 1793, and was a charter member of the Church there. By various removals they came to make their home at Madison, O , where she died May 20, 1851, in her eighty-first year. She had two daughters, and a son Alanson, who removed to Kentucky, and there had seven sons and five daughters. The eldest son, John Tarvin Gray, born 1821, married his accomplished cousin, Cynthia Raymond, granddaughter of Melissa Burritt Raymond, and became a noted civil engineer and bridge builder, and still resides at Covington, Ky. Another son, Philander Raymond Gray, was a loyal Kentuckian in the war for the Union, was afterwards Sheriff of Venango County, Pa., Collector of Internal Revenue for that district, and for several years Superintendent of the great Eclipse and Standard Oil Co. works, near Franklin, Pa. He is the father by one mother, of an interesting family of eight sons and three daughters, one of the sons bearing the name of Burritt Gray. His present residence is at Elizabeth, N. J.

Sarah Burritt, the fourth daughter, was born at Pound Ridge, Westchester County, Jan. 29, 1772, and married her cousin, Gurdon Wells, born Feb. 28, 1758, son of Hezekiah, son of Deacon Thomas, at Huntington, March 1. 1792, and removing to Lincklaen, Chenango County, N. Y., their daughter Matilda, born Aug. 9, 1800, who still survives,* a Widow Smith, at Three Rivers, Mich., was the first white child born

*—She died March 17, 1892, in her ninety-second year.

in that township. Gurdon Wells died there Dec. 27, 1827, and she died Oct. 31, 1831, in her sixtieth year. She was a very decided character, and eminent in Christian piety. It is said that a man who had heard of her, came thirty miles once to see her, hoping that she would be able to expound the way of life more perfectly unto him. But then, that was a time when people believed something and thought it of some consequence what they did believe.

Ely Burritt, the eldest son, born at Pound Ridge, March 12, 1773, graduated at Williams College in the class of 1800, was licensed to practice medicine at Troy, N. Y., March 29, 1802, and became eminent as a physician. Dr. Wayland, who studied medicine with him, says: "Dr. Burritt was a man of remarkable logical powers, of enthusiastic love of his profession, and of great and deserved confidence in his own judgment. He stood at the head of his profession in Troy, and in the neighboring region, and was a person of high moral character." He married Mehitabel Stratton, daughter of Deacon Stratton, of Williamstown, Mass., April 12, 1798. There were four sons and three daughters born to them, of whom only one son and a daughter had descendants. This son, Alexander Hamilton Burritt, born in Troy, April 17, 1805, commenced the practice of medicine in 1827, after the Alopath system, which he continued until 1838, when he embraced Homœopathy, placing himself for a time under the instruction of his distinguished kinsman, the late Dr. John F. Gray, of New York, who was a grandson of Rev. Blackleach Burritt. He then practiced the new system; first, in Crawford County, Pa. He afterwards removed to Cleveland, O., where he aided in the organization of the Western Homœopathic College in 1850, and was Vice President and Professor of Obstetrics until 1854, when he resigned on account of his health, and removing to New Orleans, was successfully engaged in practice there until his death, Oct. 1876. His son, Amatus Robbins Burritt, born in 1833, graduated from the Western Homœopathic College in 1853, engaged in practice at Huntsville, Ala. In 1866 he married Miss Mary K. Robinson, by whom he had a son, Dr. William H. Burritt, born 1869, now in practice at Huntsville, where his father died Aug. 22, 1876. Dr. A. R. Burritt was for a time in the Confederate service, while his only brother, (there is a surviving sister, Mrs. Julia A. Gary, of Evansville, Ind,) Ely Burritt, now of Fall River, Mass., was in the Union Army, and being taken prisoner, Dr. A. R, was instrumental in securing his release. This branch of the Burritt family, is remarkable in that it is represented by four generations of physicians, all of high reputation, being the son, grandson, great-grandson and great-great-grandson of Rev. Blackleach Burritt. Dr. Ely Burritt died at Troy, Sep. 1, 1823, in his fifty-first year. His widow afterwards married Professor John Adams, the noted Principal of Exeter Phillips Academy, Andover, Mass. Julia Ann Burritt, daughter of Dr. Ely, and said to have been a remarkably beautiful girl, married, Dr. Amatus Robbins, and died Dec. 12, 1839, in her nineteenth year, leaving a son who is a physician in New Haven. A tradition of Dr. Ely Burritt is, that on the capture of his father, being then a boy of six years, he threw corn cobs at the British soldiers as expressive of his patriotic indignation!

Gideon Burritt, son of Rev. Blackleach, born in Pound Ridge, Sep. 15, 1774, married Sarah Bowne, lived at Winhall and Manchester, Vt., where he died in 1858. Had ten children, of whom three still survive at Manchester, viz.: Deacon Edwin Burritt, who married Mary Chellis, and has descendants, Jared Burritt, and Hon. Johnson Burritt. A son, Ely, married Esther Strait, whose mother was Rachel Purdy, and removed to Columbia, Bradford County, Pennsylvania. Mrs. Sarah Burritt Mosher, of Albany N. Y., widow of the late Dr. C. D. Mosher, of Albany, is a daughter of Ely.

Diantha Burritt, daughter of Rev. Blackleach, born at Pound Ridge, Jan. 9, 1776, married John Gray, Jr., at Winhall, Vt., May 26, 1793. Judge John Gray was an early and prominent citizen of Sherburne, N. Y., and afterwards removed to Sheridan, Chautauqua County, where she died Oct. 14, 1846. There were six sons and two daughters born to her. Three of the sons became physicians, one of them, the late Dr. John F. Gray, pre-eminent as the first to embrace the doctrines of

Hahnemann, in the city of New York, and distinguished for his large and successful practice. Another of the sons, Rev. Blackleach Burritt Gray, was a Presbyterian Minister, and one of his sons, General John Burritt Gray, now of New York, won distinction by his services as Adjutant General of the State of Missouri, during the War of the Rebellion. A daughter, Diantha, became eminent as a teacher, and with her late husband, the Rev. H. A. Sackett, was influential in the founding of Elmira Female College, at Elmira, N. Y. This lady of rare gifts and high Christian character, whose home is at Cranford, N. J., is one of the surviving grand-children of Rev. Blackleach Burritt, whose memory she has done much to perpetuate.

Rufus Burritt, supposed to have been born in 1777, studied medicine with his brother, Dr. Ely, at Troy, and was admitted to practice in 1806. It is said that going away for a time to look about the country, he returned to find his intended married to some one else; hence he never married, and led a roving life, teaching some—and he is said to have been an excellent teacher—as he had opportunity both in Pennsylvania and Kentucky, in which latter State he died, in Campbell County, about 1850. A gifted but very eccentric man.

Blackleach Burritt, Jr., born at Pound Ridge, N. Y., Oct. 27, 1779, while his father was in the old Sugar House Prison, after the death of his mother went to Huntington, Conn., to live with his kindred, and on Nov. 1, 1802, married Sally Hubbell, daughter of John Hubbell, Jr. They removed to Pennsylvania in 1810, and he died at Wilksbarre, Oct. 1, 1830. They had two daughters and six sons, as follows:

Hepsa, born 1804; married Ziba Burns; residence, Uniondale, Susquehanna County, Pa.

Grandison, born 1806; lived in Wisconsin.

Samuel, born 1808; lived at Uniondale, Pa.

Rufus, born 1814; lived at Uniondale, Pa.

Ely, born 1817; lived at Carbondale. Pa.

Sarah Caroline, born Aug. 18, 1819; married Otis M. Dimmick, Uniondale, Pa.

Charles, born 1823; died 1825.

Samuel Burritt, third child of Blackleach, Jr., born at Huntington, Conn., March 31, 1808; married Amanda Nichols, Sep. 19, 1836; lived at Uniondale, where he died June 20, 1863. His children were:

Loren, (Col.), born June 26, 1837; died Nov. 11, 1889; married Delphine D. Raynsford.

Ira Nichols, born Dec. 28, 1838; Washington, D. C.

Philo, born April 11, 1840; lives at Uniondale.

Payson, born July 16, 1847; Kansas.

Newell, born Dec. 19, 1851.

Anna B., born July 25, 1853.

Lilian, born Feb. 16, 1858.

Colonel Loren Burritt, son of Samuel, and great grandson of Rev. Blackleach, enlisted in the Union Army as a private in Company K, Fifty-sixth Regiment Pennsylvania Volunteers, Jan. 1862. Was promoted successively to Orderly Sergeant, Second Lieutenant, First Lieutenant, and on the 2nd of July, 1863, at the Battle of Gettysburg, was assigned to duty on the Staff of General Cutler. In Nov. 1863 was commissioned Major of the Eighth Regiment, U. S. Colored Troops; was severely wounded at Olustee, Fla., Feb. 20, 1864; was promoted to Lieutenant-Colonel while in the Hospital at Beaufort, S. C.; succeeded to the command of his Regiment, in front of Petersburg; was afterward detailed at Newport News and Norfolk, Va.: was President of a Board of Inquiry to investigate the commandant of the Eastern Department of Virginia. In the Summer and Fall of 1865, was in Texas, and received his discharge in December of that year. Engaged in practice of the law for a time at Philadelphia, but suffering from his wounds broke his health, and after being an invalid for several years he died at Athens, Bradford County Pa., Nov. 11, 1889. A man of high character and attainments and a worthy descendant of his patriotic sire. He was greatly interested in his ancestry, and the genealogical statistics which he collected has added much of interest to this sketch. His widow resides at Owego, N. Y.

Mrs. S. C. Dimmick, of Uniondale, Pa., is a daughter of Blackleach, Jr., and a grand-daughter of Rev. Blackleach Burritt.

Prudence Burritt, next to the youngest daughter of Rev. Blackleach Burritt, born at Huntington, Nov. 2, 1782, married in Oct. 1802, James Welles, son of Josiah, son of Hezekiah; lived at Edmeston, Otsego County, N. Y., then at Portage, Livingston County, N. Y., where he died Aug. 26, 1848, and she died March 13, 1852. A son, Delos C. Welles, of Monticello, Minn., and two daughters, Mrs. Semantha Wilcox, and Mrs. L. C. Britain, of Sodus, N. Y., still survive.

Samuel Burritt, the youngest son, born about 1784, was a protege of Miss Susannah DeLancey, who seems to have cared for him after the death of his mother, in 1786. He studied law, for a time acted as agent for a part of the DeLancey estate, and died in the city of New York in 1820, leaving two children who died unmarried.

Susannah Burritt, was born at Red Mills, modern Mahopac Falls, Putnam County, N. Y., March 5, 1786, just six weeks before her mother's death. Believing her illness to be fatal, it is said that Mrs. Burritt sent for Miss Susannah DeLancey, the unmarried daughter of Lieutenant-Governor DeLancey, who lived at nearby Crompond, who despite powerful family influence remained true to the cause of the Colonies, and was a warm friend of the Burritt family. On her dying bed she gave her infant daughter to Miss DeLancey's keeping, and she was faithful to the trust. Bringing her up carefully as her own child, she willed her a considerable estate,—a farm of 129 acres in Yorktown, Westchester County, N. Y., and all her personal estate, including a Negro Slave,"Hannah." Susannah Burritt, named after her benefactress, married Elijah Fowler, in 1804, who died in 1812, leaving two sons, one of whom, Samuel Burritt Fowler, now resides at Putnam Valley, Putnam County, N. Y. She married second, Charles Adams, Dec. 1821, and had a daughter Charlotte, born in 1823, who married George W. Seeley, and resides at Lansing, Mich. Mrs. Susannah Burritt Adams, died at Bristol, Ind., Sept. 19, 1881, in her ninety-sixth year, the oldest as well as the youngest of her mother's twelve children.

Deborah Burritt, the first child by the second marriage,

must have been born as early as 1791, as her father makes
mention of her in that year. She was taken to Sherburne
soon after her father's death, there married Milo Hatch,
and died Oct. 11, 1851. Had four sons, of whom three survive: Wells Burritt Hatch, of Syracuse, N. Y., Watson A., of
Loyd, Wis., and Albert R. Hatch, of Greeley, Col.

In regard to the youngest child and son of Rev. Blackleach Burritt, the following is copied from the old Church
records, of Winhall, Vt.: "March the 3d. A. D., 1793, was baptized Selah Wells, the son of the Rev. Mr. Blackleach, and
Deborah Burritt." The following inscription from the memorial stone at his grave in Sherburne, N. Y., shows how he
was cut down while yet in the bloom of youth:

"Selah Wells Burritt, youngest son of Rev. Blackleach
Burritt, and only son of Deborah Burritt, died Nov. 19th,
in the 18th year of his age."

"Insatiate Archer, could'st thou not spare to riper age the virtuous
youth,
The widow's only hope, the staff of her declining years?"

In view of his widowed mother's helplessness, in her old
age this seems an almost prophetic as well as sad lament.

This interesting group of Rev. Blackleach Burritt's descendants of fourteen children and sixty grand-children, fourteen
of the latter of whom still survive, might well form the theme
of an interesting paper, but must be passed by without further notice here. He certainly had prolific posterity as well
as a virile ancestry.

But to return to his father, Peleg Burritt, Jr.: It is said
that within a reasonable time after the death of Peleg's
first wife, his mother made a quilting party, to which she in-
vited all the eligible young people of the neighborhood, and
among them, Deborah Beardslee. She recommended Deborah
as the most sensible of the girls; and Peleg took her for his
second wife. The marriage took place at Ripton Parish, "on
the evening of Thanksgiving Day," as the record says, in 1746.
She was born at Stratford, Feb. 1, 1726, and was the great-
granddaughter of Richard Booth and Elizabeth Hawley his
wife, of Stratford as early as 1640.

Peleg Burritt, Jr., took the Freeman's oath April 13, 1741 ; is mentioned as Peleg Burritt, Junior, several times from 1752 to 1761, in the Society records of Ripton. At a meeting held at his house Dec. 6, 1752, he was chosen Clerk, and sworn for the year ensuing. Was also Clerk in 1753-4. In 1773-4, he is said to have joined the Connecticut Colony in the Wyoming Valley, taking up his residence in the township of Hanover, now in Luzerne County, Pa.

"Hanover Green" was laid out in old New England style containing an open court or green, flanked on two sides by the homes of two of the children of Captain Peleg Burritt, Stephen and Sarah, each with its symmetrical front yard, garden, orchard, &c., while the green was open to the street at the front, and occupied at the rear by a Church, back of which was a Cemetery. The whole establishment was laid out by the Burritt family; whether by Captain Peleg Burritt or his son Stephen, is not known. But all this happy scene was broken in upon by the terrible tragedy of the Wyoming Massacre, which occurred the 3d day of July, 1778, and in which Cyprian Hibbard, a son-in-law of Peleg Burritt, husband of his daughter Sarah, was killed. Although Mr. Burritt was not in the Wyoming Valley at the date of the battle, his wife Deborah, was there, and rendered efficient aid during the escape of the fugitives. It is related that all the books and papers belonging to the Burritt's were hastily thrown into a bag, as the result of the battle became known, and that inasmuch as the first thought was to escape by way of the river to Shamokin, the bag was hastily thrown into a boat in which some of the refugees did so make their escape, and thus went down the river without anyone to care for it ; since the Burritt's changed their plan, and escaped, with many others, to the east, over the mountains, to the Delaware river. The important consignment was afterwards traced as far as Shamokin or Northumberland, but after that was lost sight of. And thus were lost the only records and papers of this branch of the Burritt family, brought from their early home in Connecticut.

It is related that Mrs. Burritt, on the hasty retreat, had

the forethought to throw upon her horse a bag of flour; and that was the sole sustenance of a considerable party, on their flight to the Delaware. On camping at night, or halting for refreshment, she would form the meal into a cup shape in the mouth of the bag, and pouring in water, would mix up the meal into dough, and bake it upon the coals. It is impossible now to find out who formed the Burritt contingent in this retreat. Mrs. B.'s husband is supposed to have been at the time absent, probably in Connecticut. It is fair to presume that all of their children may have been present in the valley at the time, yet one or more of them may have been with their father in Connecticut.

The following is a partial list of the descendants of Peleg Burritt, Jr., by his second marriage:

Gideon, unmarried, died in Hanover township, Luzerne County, Pa.

Sarah, born Nov. 19, 1750; married first Cyprian Hibbard, Jan., 1775; second, Matthias Hollenback, who was an officer in the Battle of Wyoming, and escaped from the massacre by swimming the river. He was entitled Colonel Hollenback. Sarah Burritt, had by her first husband, Hannah D., born June 18, 1788; being thus fifteen days old at the time of the battle and massacre of Wyoming, in which her father, (Cyprian Hibbard), was killed. She married John Alexander and had three children.

Thomas, died in infancy.

Sarah, died in infancy.

William H. Alexander, married Caroline Ulp; Miss E. I. Alexander of Wilksbarre, is of one their six children.

Sarah Burritt had by her second husband, Judge Matthias Hollenback:

1. Mary Ann, married Laning; three sons and three daughters. One of her grand-children was Mrs. Anthony J. Drexel, of Philadelphia.

2. Ellen J., born Jan. 21, 1788; married Charles F. Welles, born at Glastonbury, Conn., 1789, son of John Welles, of Glastonbury, born 1756; son of John, born 1729; son of Thomas, born 1693; son of Captain Samuel, born at Wethers-

field, 1660; son of Samuel, born in England, 1630; son of Governor Thomas Welles. There were nine children by this marriage, of whom Rev. H. H. Welles, graduate of Princeton, '44, of Kingston, Pa, and Edward Welles, Esq., of Wilkes-Barre, are two of the six surviving.

3. Sarah Hollenback, married first Jacob Cist; second, Chester Butler; seven children.

4. George M. Hollenback, Wilkes-Barre, born Aug. 11, 1791, married twice, and died Nov., 1866; no children.

Mr. Charles F. Welles was a man of large property in coal lands.

Stephen Burritt, son of Peleg. Jr., married a Miss Keeler, and had Joel, who married Ruth, and had numerous descendants, including a grand-son Joel, now of White Haven, Pa. Also Stephen, had a son Stephen, Jr., who may have had descendants, and a daughter Polly, who married a Mr. Dilley, and was the mother of Rev. Alex. B. Dilley, of Florida.

Mary, the youngest daughter of Peleg Burritt, Jr., was twice married but left no children. Captain Peleg Burritt, as he was sometimes called, died at Hanover Green, Pa., April 10, 1789, and his widow, Deborah, at the same place, Aug. 7, 1802.

Characterization of Rev. Blackleach Burritt is not wanting. He is said to have been a little visionary and unpractical, but very pious and devoted. He was strong and earnest in debate, and as evidence of his controversial powers, it is related of him, that meeting a brother minister one evening on the highway, and getting into a discussion with him on some theological, doctrinal point, they continued there, sitting on horseback, until the dawn of the next morning! He possessed wonderful physical strength and agility, and at College was noted for such feats. As a preacher, he was distinguished for readiness and a love of argument. He preached a great deal extemporaneously, and would sometimes take a text handed to him, as he went into the pulpit, and preach from it without any previous preparation. He was a very thoughtful man, a student; but so occupied with his reflections, and the study of life and immortality, as to be almost indifferent to ordinary mundane matters. It is said that with his other gifts he had a glorious voice for singing, and that it almost carried one away to hear him in some of the grand old anthems.

The following extracts from a letter of Rev. Blackleach Burritt to his sister, Mrs. Sarah Hollenback, wife of Colonel Matthias Hollenback, of Wilkes-Barre, Pa., now in the possession of Miss E. I. Alexander, of that place, and the only letter of his known to be in existence, is a striking self characterization:

Duanes Borough, N. Y., December 28. A. D. 1791.

DEAR SISTER: Your Relations in this Place are generally in good Health, except myself who for a length of Time have been more feeble & Disordered than usual. . . Stiles Wells has lately Returned from Huntington (alias Ripton), & informs (me) that our Friend(s) are in good Health there. . . Brother Hubbell & Sister were well last Spring, Since which Time I have not heard from them. . . I know not but you are ready to Imagine I am forgetful of you & my Mother & Brethren in Wyoming, as I have not Wrote to any of them, since I Received your Kind Letter Informing me of the Death of Father, which was the First Certain Intelligence I obtained of his Death. "Our Fathers, where are they? and the Prophets, do they live forever?" We are hastening to follow them; a few more Revolving Suns brings us to the concluding Scene of all Earthly Joys & Sorrows; we momentarily hasten to the House appointed for all the Living.

I am not unmindful of you, & my Relations so remarkably Scattered from Each other, as I am almost Daily praying for them, in my Family, & many Times conversing of you & them; but it is Rare that we have any opportunity of Conveying Letters from this Quarter of the Country to where you Dwell. I desire to embrace every opportunity of Writing to you in my Power, & wish you & my Friends near you would Do the Same in letting us hear from them. I greatly wish to hear of the State of Religion in Wyomen in General, where Discord hath so greatly abounded in years past, & whether they obtain Regular Presbyterian or congregational Settled Ministers in the towns in general, what Success there is of the Preaching of the Gospel in your Part of the Country, as there is but little visible good Effect of the Preaching of the Gospel in general in the Northern Part of this State. — Real Godliness is the All Important Concern, without which nothing will Serve our Turn in the Hour of Death, or in the future Judgment, to which we are swiftly Hastening. Temporal Prosperity, & External Privileges, while Zion languishes, and the Interest of that glorious Kingdom that will finally brake in peaces all the Kingdoms that have opposed it, & stand forever, is visibly Di___ b I ___ ___ ___ __ ___ Part of the land, but little Satisfies. — I am greatly ___ ___ ___ ___ my Friends at Turns, least Prosperity, or ___ ___ ___ ___ ___ ___ __ ___ them in Destruction & perdition. Prosperity is ___ ___ ___ far more Dangerous than Adversity to Christians in Every Age __ why should I fear? Since Zion's Glorious King Reigns in wisdom, Righteousness & Goodness, & is ever Accomplishing the noblest Ends by the wisest & Best of ALL possible Means. We may fear for them, in a partial View; tho' in the most large & Extensive View, there is the utmost Reason of Rejoicing in the Absolute perfection of the Divine Government, or Disposal of Events in Providence.—

Perhaps you may have an opportunity of Writing to me by Mr. John Gray, the young Man who is the Bearer hereof, a Neighbor of mine, on his Return to Dannesborough.— Pray give my Dutiful Regards to Mother, & let her know I often think of her in her lonely condition; my youngest Child is of her Name.— Give my love (if you Please,) to All My Brethren & yrs. and my unknown Brother will have a share among the Rest. The Bearer is waiting. I must Subscribe myself, Your Effectionate Brother,

Blackleach Burritt.

It has been stated that his grave at Winhall was unmarked. It should be added in explanation that several years since a sum was contributed to furnish a stone for that purpose, but by some misdirection it was placed at Manchester, eight miles away over the Green Mountains, on the plot of one of his descendants there. The following is the inscription upon it:

REV. BLACKLEACH BURRITT,

Born at Stratford, Ct., 17—,

Died at Winhall, Vt., 1794.

"An earnest Minister of the Gospel, a learned and upright man, His spotless memory is piously cherished by his descendants."

A son of Fairfield County and of your own Stratford, he well deserves a place in your annals, and is worthy to be held in honored remembrance by his kindred and descendants

NOTE.—Acknowledgement is made for kindly aid in the preparation of this paper, to Rev. Samuel Orcutt, the Historian of Stratford; to R. B. Lacey, Esq., President of the Fairfield County Historical Society; Rev. W. J. Cumming, of Yorktown, N. Y.; Edward Welles, Esq., of Wilkes-Barre, Pa., Mrs. Col. Loren Burritt, of Owego, N. Y.; Mrs. D. E. Sackett, Cranford, N. J.; Mrs. C. D. Mosher, Albany, N. Y., and many others.   M. D. R.

Rev. Samuel Mills, son of Rev. Jedediah Mills, and class-mate of Rev. Mr. Burritt, referred to in the foregoing pages, as of Bedford, Westchester County, from 1769, having been ordained as pastor of the Church there, Dec. 13, of that year, remained there until by the stress of the Revolution he was obliged in 1779, to remove to Fredricksburg, North Society, now Patterson, Putnam County, and did not return to Bedford after the close of the war, though strongly urged to do so. In 1789 he became an Ana-Baptist, and so severed his relations with the Dutchess County Presbytery. He soon after removed to the Geneseo country, locating at Williams-burg, between Geneseo and Mt. Morris. He was a pioneer preacher in that region, and his memory was long cherished in that locality, for his worth and devoted piety. He died in 1813, and was buried in the Geneseo cemetery. His widow, second wife, was a sister of Colonel Daniel Humphrey, an aides-de-camp of Washington. He left four sons, viz: Alex-ander, Lewis F., Philo and William Augustus Mills, the latter of whom born in Bedford, May 27, 1777, located at Mt. Morris, Livingston County, N. Y. Was Major-General in the War of 1812-15, Supervisor twenty years, a man of great en-terprise, a large landed proprietor and active member of the Presbyterian Church, died April 6, 1844. He had ten chil-dren, of whom Myron Holly Mills, born Dec. 8, 1820, re-sides at Mt. Morris, N. Y. He graduated at the Geneva Medical College in 1844, was Assistant Surgeon U. S. Army in the Mexican war ; was in practice at Rochester from 1850 to 1870, was one of the founders of the Livingston County Historical Society, President of the Board of Education and of the Mills Water Works, author of a series of articles on Indian History, has delivered many addresses, lectures, &c., and held various positions of honor and trust. Another son, Rev. Samuel J. Mills, of Nevada, Iowa, graduated at Yale in 1837, was for a time engaged in practice of the law, and has been engaged in the ministry since 1859.

www.ingramcontent.com/pod-product-compliance
Lightning Source LLC
Chambersburg PA
CBHW021246260626
47172CB00002B/867